BACKPAGE'S BEST

Copyright © 2022 by K.T. Thompson

All rights reserved. In accordance with the U.S. Copyright Act of 1976, the scanning, uploading, and electronic sharing of any part of this book without permission of the publisher constitute unlawful piracy and theft of the author's intellectual property. If you would like to use material from the book (other than for review purposes), prior written permission.

Thank you for your support of the author's rights.

VMH ™ Publishing
3355 Lenox Rd. NE Suite 750
Atlanta, GA 30326
www.vmhpublishing.com

The publisher is not responsible for websites, or social media pages (or their content) related to this publication, that are not owned by the publisher. Quantity sales. Special discounts are available on quantity purchases by corporations, associations, and others.

Paperback ISBN: 978-1-0880-7361-2

Ebook ISBN: 978-1-0880-7363-6

This is a work of fiction. Names, characters, businesses, places, events, locales, and incidents are either the products of the author's imagination or used in a fictitious manner. Any resemblance to actual persons, living or dead, or actual events is purely coincidental.

BACKPAGE'S BEST

Written by:

K.T. Thompson

Contents

Three Years Later Pervy Paul vii

Chapter 1 : Maxximum exposure................................1

Chapter 2 : Soul Train line..7

Chapter 3 : Too weak 13

Chapter 4 : Simping ain't easy..................................23

Chapter 5 : Jackson Center reunion 27

Chapter 6 : Eastside story 37

Chapter 7 : The Feds are watching 49

Chapter 8 : It was so crazy that it had to be true 55

Chapter 9 : Beware of Dawg 61

Chapter 10 : We check paperwork cause paperwork don't lie 67

Chapter 11 : Go feed my friends 75

Three Years Later

PERVY PAUL

PAUL ARCHIBALD IS SITTING AT his desk at work, deep in thought. Paul wasn't thinking or worrying about the task at hand of operating in his best capacity as principal at this prominent, affluent private school in Winter Park Florida. He was too busy thinking about calling that young sexy Black chick named Janay. He had been calling and happily paying her to help remove some of the stress from being a principal, a man, and married. Winter Park is a nice abundant city on the outskirts of Orlando filled with mansions and manicured lawns covering much of its landscape. Paul had been the principal at this particular school for twelve years now. He had been married to his wife, Melanie, for twenty-two years. They had met twenty-four years ago when they were both teachers at a junior high school in Altamonte Springs, Florida. It's ironic that they both had been caught up in the same curriculum overhaul that had affected Janay and thousands of other students in the region. But in spite of a whole bunch of well-hidden and disguised problems, they stayed together like the Isley Brothers.

They had three kids ages sixteen, fourteen, and ten. After the birth of their last child, they both decided that it would be best if Melanie became a stay-at-home mom. She'd stay home and give up her career as a teacher handling three kids and the household. While Paul worked long grueling hours as a principal making the money to keep all of the bills paid. Much like a lot of long-term marriages, Paul and Melanie had found themselves in a marriage of convenience. It was more convenient for them to stay together and keep up appearances, than it was for them to split up and go their separate ways.

They both no longer loved each other, but their kids, in-laws, and friends had no idea of this because they were both A-list actors when it came to it. They hadn't had sexual intercourse in a number of years, because it seems that they let that fire go out after their last child was born. Melanie felt that over the course of time her husband's sexual appetite had begun to get weirder and more vulgar, requesting things that weren't even on the menu. His sexual requests had gone from basic to bizarre. They had survived all these years together on Kama Sutra sex. Now all of a sudden he was into kink. She wondered where he had learned this filth that he was requesting in their bedroom. He would ask her to do vile things to him, like spit on him, choke him, slap him around, and even urinate on him.

She felt like choking him and slapping him around after his attempt to involve her in his debauchery, but not in a sexual way. Just like millions of repressed, fed-up, lonely married women all throughout the world, she stayed with him to keep up the façade of one big happy family for the sake of her kids. She wasn't doing this Oscar Award-winning acting performance for Paul's perverted ass, that's for damn sure. Unlike millions of repressed, fed-up, lonely married women throughout the world, Melanie had a plan B. No not the morning-after pill many women were popping to avoid an unwanted pregnancy. Her plan B was a well-thought-out and planned escape from her marriage to a man she had irreconcilable differences with.

She was just hanging around until after all of her children were out of the house and away at college. She and Paul had both agreed to file separate divorce petitions and go their separate ways. But for now she was taking one for the team. She was living an outright lie, again just like millions of unhappily married women all throughout the world. Divorce or separation would do a number of things, most of them not good for her best interests. Divorce or separation would derail her opulent lifestyle. She had given up her career as an educator a long time ago to become a homebody housewife. For a long period of time now her main priority had been to take care of the kids and the house. Lord knows her decision had by no means been easy. Her situation was like a person reluctantly taking a group photo, pausing, turning, and posing for an inconsiderate photographer who kept messing up the shots. So she'd be forced to keep doing it again and again, over and over.

Their sex life was nonexistent outside of frequent acts of public displays of affection when they were out. She cringed at the thought of him actually touching her in a sexual way again. But for now she was being a model inmate, doing her time. Counting down the days until she got out of this prison. Paul came and went as he pleased. The agreement he and Melanie made to help keep up appearances was that he would show up for important family functions. She had access to their considerably large joint bank account. She paid the bills, balanced the checkbook, went grocery and clothes shopping for the whole household, and looked after, took care of, and provided for the kids.

Yeah, she'd just go ahead and play her role as the naïve little housewife. Playing the fool to a man who thought that he had all the good cards in the deck. A man that also thought that God had given him all the sense, and everybody else almost none. Melanie had also heard that song before "Everybody Plays the Fool" by the group Main Ingredient. She hummed it while in the laundry room of their large house washing a load of her children's clothes. A large toothy smile appeared across her face as she hummed her motivational theme song "Dawg on the Loose."

A large thick-necked, big-shouldered, big-handed man in his mid-twenties is sitting at a kitchen table at one of his many secret locations. He's sitting there counting a huge stack of money that was just dropped off to him a few minutes ago by two of his lieutenants. He's wearing his crew's signature, customary, legendary attire. A sort of team uniform of a fishermen's hat with matching in color sneakers. Shayy Dawg had gotten out of juvenile detention on his eighteenth birthday and two years later he had ascended to their alpha male and leader. After he took over, Tarver Court became a no-fly zone, meaning the crap that people could get away with in other neighborhoods, that wasn't flying by in Beirut Boys territory.

By now formally violent gangs such as The Smurfs, The Grimlins, The Motown Boys, The Chill Town Boys, Carver Shores, Lake Mann, and Mercy Drive had all disbanded or ceased to exist. Each and every one of those former gangs had neighborhood territories in West Orlando that they hung out in and terrorized. Smurfs roamed the Johnson Village section of West Orlando. The Grimlins roamed Ivey Lane and Malibu. The Motown Boys roamed Mercheson Terrace. The Lake Mann Boys roamed and hung out in a large apartment complex built right off the lake. The Chill Town Boys roamed a large neighborhood of family homes called Richmond Heights. The Carver Shores Boys roamed a large neighborhood of family homes with the same name.

And last but not least was Mercy Drive. There was no Mercy Drive Boys, because they never officially formed a gang. But Mercy Drive was the second most notorious area in Orlando after Beirut. It was filled with renegades all from different neighborhoods who would band together and join forces anytime in the main apartment complex they all lived, sold drugs, robbed, boosted, and gambled in. The name of the apartment complex was The Palms and you had to know someone who knew someone or something to regularly come and hang over there. All of these gangs were now long gone, except the Beirut Boys. All of these neighborhoods had been infiltrated and used as storehouses or trap houses, except Tarver Court. Shayy Dawg had come up through the ranks. He had been a runner for this gang. He had been a watch-out for this gang. He had been a mule. He had been an enforcer. He had been a shooter. He knew about and believed in loyalty. He was a young thirteen-year-old boy when he came and joined this gang. He was almost twenty-six years old, which meant that he had been in this gang for almost half of his life.

Now he was a battle-tested young man who ruled his turf with an iron fist. He was the general of the strongest and only ship still floating in West Orlando. He wasn't about to allow the Beirut Boys and Tarver Court to sink on his watch. He was an opposing figure of a man. He stood six foot one and weighed 250 solid pounds. Wide shoulders, big arms, and abnormally large hands. There was a truth said about him jokingly that he could grab a man so tight with his hands, that to get the man loose someone would have to come along and cut him out of his grip. Then there was the story still out there floating around about him beating up the four guys who were trying to jump him into the gang. He had been running the Beirut Boys now close to four years, but ever since he took over, he ran it like a well-oiled machine with many different moving parts.

The Beirut Boys we're now a street gang that operated like a business. Shayy Dawg wasn't just a leader of a vicious group of warriors who wore fishermen's hats and matching sneakers. He was also an intelligent, shrewd businessman.

Chapter 1

MAXXIMUM EXPOSURE

ORLANDO WAS A RAPIDLY GROWING city in the early '90s. One of the main reasons for this was that it had mainly become a two-sided city. There is a West Orlando and an East Orlando. Both sides are vastly different in race, heritage, and culture. But both were growing rapidly in population, mainly the Eastside. Both separated by I-4 and Downtown Orlando. Once you were going in either direction, if you crossed under I-4 you were either in West or East Orlando. In the 1990s East Orlando had begun to separate itself in stature from West Orlando. East Orlando began to become the nicer, newer section of the two sides. Many of the upper-class White and Black families, who had previously resided in nice safe neighborhoods in West Orlando were relocating to nice new gated communities with manicured lawns in East Orlando.

Before the Eastside was renovated and opened up, mainly Hispanics such as Puerto Ricans, Mexicans, Dominicans, and Cubans called East Orlando home. During those early decades, East Orlando was mainly thousands and thousands of acres of orange groves and woods. But once UCF, the second largest college in America, stopped playing their home football games at the old Citrus Bowl and built their own stadium on their campus in East Orlando, it seemed like a diametric shift happened in Orlando. West Orlando had always been the tough crime-ridden section. As the Eastside opened up and got bigger, crime began to take hold on the entire city. Crimes that usually were solved in a nice timely manner were now being long, drawn-out affairs.

It got so bad, Orlando, which had two large local levels of law enforcement, a Police Department and a Sheriff's Office, began begging the public and its citizens for help with campaign's like 423-TIPS. If you see something, say something, Crimeline and Whistleblowers. The crime rate went up. The murder rate went up. Drugs had flooded the Central Florida streets, and many old cases were transferred over to a cold-case division. As the city of Orlando grew, so did the smaller surrounding cities, such as Apopka, Eatonville, Winter Park, Altamonte Springs, Winter Garden, and Sanford. The Sheriff's Office helped patrol most of those small cities, which all had their own separate set of crime problems too. There were also huge differences when it came to West Orlando and East Orlando; anyone who lived there or visited there for any significant amount of time could attest to that. The Westside had The Trail a world-famous stroll where women came from all over the world for prostitution purposes. The Eastside had the Alafaya Trail with new paved roads and lined with houses inside of gated communities and brand-new strip malls.

Maxximillian Otero resided in East Orlando. He was a smooth talking, flashy dressing mover and shaker who had his hand in on many hustles in the East Orlando streets. He had started out petty hustling—selling a little weed, cocaine, and pills. Then he expanded to acquiring a gambling house that brought in a lot of revenue. Inside of that gambling house they played Poker, Tonk, Spades, and they Skinned. He also ran dice games, dominoes, bet on sporting events, and played this numbers game called Bolita. Maxx had catered cooked food, drinks, and plenty of alcoholic beverages such as beer, wine, and liquor there so that his customers could gamble, eat, drink, or whatever without having to get up and leave and go and get those things.

He even had some very attractive, fine, scantily clad girls there serving the food and drinks. His gambling house and having the nearly naked girls was such a success, it led Maxx to opening up a strip club. He had become known as a person to go see in East Orlando if you needed or wanted something. He didn't stop there. He went on to open up a salon, a barbershop, and a tattoo parlor. He spent most of his time between the gambling house and the strip club, because those were two of his weaknesses. Gambling and women, and those two establishments bought in the most money. He didn't have a girlfriend or a main lady or anything like that, but he hardly ever slept alone. He didn't do anything outside of smoke a little weed and drink liquor occasionally. And although he had people who sold drugs for him, he didn't use hard drugs. But he did occasionally sample the many different women who worked at his establishments.

Even though there were now many gangs in East Orlando, such as the Latin Kings who were very well represented in that area, he wasn't in a gang, nor was he interested in joining one. Maxx was the type of person who liked giving orders, not taking them. He was too busy making money and overseeing his many business ventures. He could be seen regularly driving around town in his loud green Range Rover truck. That's the way a lot of people on the Eastside recognized him, by that loud green expensive SUV he drove and nicknamed Slimer from the old *Ghostbusters* movies. He was well known, well respected, and grudgingly liked on the Eastside of Orlando. That's the problem most people run into in large two-sided cities.

When Maxx would sparingly travel to the Westside of Orlando, he found that he was just another strange new face. He didn't get the red carpet treatment that he usually got on the Eastside. Back in the old days in Orlando before they opened the Eastside up like double doors, Orlando wasn't a city that you could easily get lost in. One reason was because everyone knew everyone. But now in these new times, it had become a large two-sided city, where if you wanted to get lost and not be found, you just simply switched sides.

Chapter 2

SOUL TRAIN LINE

THE SOUL TRAIN WAS A very popular nationally syndicated television show in the '70s, '80s, and '90s in the African American communities. It highlighted all of the latest fads, dance moves, movies, clothing, and lingo of hipster African American people. One of the main highlights of the show was when they would all line up, men on one side and women on the other, with a huge space in between themselves, as a man and a woman each put on a display of dance moves spectacularly dancing down the Soul Train Line. Pervy Paul and his close friend Jude, who was a circuit court and juvenile judge had their own version of the Soul Train Line going on in Central Florida.

In religious circles a Soul Train was a vessel or vehicle used to store and transport souls to Hell. Judge Jude and Pervy Paul were partners in crime, and their crime was to illegally cheat the juvenile justice court system. Judge Jude would illegally detain poor and underprivileged children, locking them up and making it hard for them to get out. Many of them, he would harshly over-sentence so that they could spend more time in juvenile detention centers, jails, work-release centers, or work camps. These kids were being used for free and cheap labor of the large corporations that paid Judge Jude and Pervy Paul under the table.

Pervy Paul's role consisted of him reporting at risk, low-income, poor, and destitute students to Judge Jude and the many wardens of the work-release camps, work camps, and juvenile detention centers. Being that he was a principal, he had access to sensitive documents and personal information about many students in Central Florida. He had addresses. He had financial status. He knew whose parents were divorced, or still together. He had much-needed and useable information that helped make everything that they were doing a bit easier. In Orlando and all over the nation, private prisons were running a pay-for-play scam of supply and demand. The supply was young teenage inmates, who willingly worked for pennies on the dollar, and gained time for earlier release dates. The demand was the many new juvenile detention centers, work-release centers, work camps, and work farms, that sought out this cheap labor for a higher return.

Private prisons we're popping up like Air B&Bs all over the country, and Orlando, nicknamed The City Beautiful, was no exception. Along with all of the state-run prisons that had already been operating for over 100 years, private prisons and juvenile justice correctional institutions had all built new state-of-the-art facilities in the Central Florida region. Whenever a new private facility opened up, they immediately start vying for inmates to fill the many empty beds inside their facility. Most don't know this but jails, prisons, work-release centers, work camps, work farms, and private prisons all receive $211 dollars a day, per bed that has a living breathing body in it. They don't get paid for empty beds.

Many of those same correctional institutions have been promised by the city, county, or state that they built these facilities in that the facilities will stay filled to capacity, or at least to 90%. It has gotten so ugly that just a few years ago a private prison in Arizona filed a class-action lawsuit against the state of Arizona for not having enough inmates in the facility, nor remaining at or near 90% capacity. Also in the lawsuit, the private prison claimed that the states of Hawaii, Kansas, and Nevada also incarcerated inmates in the private prison in Arizona. Which meant that many of the inmates that were locked up and doing time in Arizona, had never been to or committed a crime there. Sadly, many of these inmates didn't get visitation from their families on a consistent basis, being that they were so far from home.

Both Judge Jude and Pervy Paul are off from work and anxiously waiting at a meeting place they both always look forward to visiting. Every two weeks, they meet together at this Chili's in Kissimmee, Florida. They're always anxious because twice a month they meet and get envelopes filled with cash from one of the wardens of a private prisons, work releases, or other correctional institution. They never knew which warden was coming to meet them and grease their palms. They didn't care either. While waiting for whoever was coming that time to get there, they would have drinks, laugh, and talk about how easy it was making that extra money. Judge Jude didn't really consider Pervy Paul to be his friend. He just tolerated him because of the easy money that they were making together.

In fact he found him quite disgusting, knowing that he had a weird fetish type obsession for young girls, sneaking around snooping and peep-tomming at that private school he was principal of. This was the type of scumbag threat he should have been getting paid under the table to sell up the river. Not the wet behind the ears kids he was about to receive an envelope filled with cash for. He would never tell Pervy Paul how he felt to his face, though. But if anyone with similar charges were to ever come before him and be found guilty. He would make that person pay for everything that Pervy Paul had bragged to him about getting away with. He would give his ass the high end of the sentencing guidelines. He would maybe hide his child molester ass from society.

On the flip side, Pervy Paul liked Judge Jude a lot. He thought that it was so cool and convenient to have an actual presiding judge as an ally. He loved the money they made together. He especially loved being able to follow, hang around, and stalk young girls undetected almost every day. Heck, to him the money was extra icing on the cake. He would stalk and follow young girls for free. All of a sudden, the warden of the new juvenile justice center in Sanford came walking through the door and over to their table. He slid in the booth next to Judge Jude. He and most of the rest of the wardens also thought ill of Pervy Paul. They all talked about him behind his back. But they all knew and agreed that he was a necessary evil who was helping to fill a huge need.

Judge Jude and Pervy Paul were helping to keep all of these wardens' facilities at over 90% capacity. The Sanford Warden ordered a glass of water from their passing waiter. As the waiter walked away to go and retrieve the glass of water, the warden slid both of them envelopes filled with cash. The Sanford Warden told the both of them how happy and satisfied he and all the rest of the wardens we're with them. The waiter came back with his glass of water, put it on the table in front of him and slid it to him. She then walked away because she had other tables to check on and attend to. The Sanford Warden picked the glass up took a very small sip from it, then put the glass back on the table in front of him. He then told Judge Jude and Pervy Paul to keep up the good work and walked out.

Jude and Paul both tucked their bulky envelopes into their pockets without counting it or looking at it. They both knew that the warden's money was good. They knew that they were working with some people whose money was probably longer than I-4. They both ordered another drink for the road, left a large tip for their waiter. Then they got up and went to their cars, to head back to their wives, who would never see or hear about the large envelopes filled with money.

Chapter 3

TOO WEAK

LISA WAS HAVING A VERY rough day, in fact the whole past week had been a complete hellhole for her. Her man, Malcolm, was on his yearly two-week family vacation with his wife and kids. Every year around the same time, he and his wife put in for family vacation time. Lisa laughed at that one because she knew his ass didn't have no damn job. His stupid ass wife was the damn fool who didn't know Lisa continued. Malcolm's wife chose different locations she wanted to fly out to every year. Last year it was Aruba. Lisa was waiting for Malcolm to call to find out where they had flown to this year. The only problem with that was during vacation trips, Malcolm would always call her from strange unknown phone numbers, because of some strange stupid family rule of no phones.

His wife would collect everyone's phone at the airport. She'd then power them all off and put them all in the same locker. Lisa knew all about Malcolm's wife, and Malcolm's wife knew all about Lisa and her bastard son. She didn't feel threatened by that power-head, project hoe. She was the one with Malcolm's last name, the big four-bedroom, three-bath house in Tangelo Park, the nice car, all of her children had Malcolm's last name, were beneficiaries on his life insurance policy. She was clearly winning when it came to Malcolm, not ghetto girl. That bitch and her bastard son stood to get nothing if something were to happen to her husband. She honestly couldn't see what her husband saw in the ghetto-fied hoodrat bitch.

Lisa thought that she was going to lose her damn mind. She didn't have her man here. She was out of drugs and she still had to make it through the rest of the week until he came back next week. She hated this time of year when that hefty bitch that he had married would kidnap him and force them apart from each other for fourteen days. Although this funky-ass vacation crap came around every year, Lisa still couldn't quite prepare herself for it. Malcolm had left her some money and personal-usage drugs, but she had run through both of them quicker than she anticipated. Malcolm had spoiled her. She was so used to him coming to her rescue and getting her by on a daily basis. It was glaringly sad how codependent she had become of him. She came to realize that his drugs were not the only thing that she was seriously addicted to.

Just as she was thinking that her cell phone began to vibrate in her pocket. She pulled it out and hoped to not see a saved programmed number, but a strange, unsaved number appeared. It said "out of area call." She quickly answered. She didn't normally answer her phone for out-of-area callers, but her man was damn sure out of the area at the time. She knew this had to be her man calling; she could just feel it. Then a voice came on the line and said your car's extended warranty is about to expire. Lisa damn near jumped through the phone line at whoever this bad-timing-ass telemarketer was.

She said, "Bitch, I ain't even got no damn car," and was just about to hang up on this idiot so hard that they would feel it. When she heard the unmistakable Eddie Murphy-like laugh of her man, Malcolm. She immediately perked up as if she had been given an extra frothy cappuccino espresso. She said, "Malcolm that crap ain't that damn funny. Now, bae, you know you're wrong for that." He continued to chuckle like Eddie on the prank he had just pulled on her.

He finally simmered down and asked, "What's up, Lisa? I was just calling to check in on you."

Lisa, minus the truth said, "Everything's good. She couldn't let him know that she was bouncing off the walls in her house, trying to remain sane. This time a little truth, so she added, "But I miss you and can't wait for you to get back."

He said, "I will be back next week, and when we get back next week you know your house will be my first stop, after I get her and the kids home.

Lisa replied, "So my house will be your second stop, then."

Malcolm caught that slight and said, "Girl, don't start that nitpicking crap. You know what I meant."

Scolded like a mannish child, Lisa said, "You're right, baby. I ain't trying to start nothing. I just miss you."

Malcolm said, "You better, and don't be having no men and them gossiping A-holes around that house either."

Lisa said, "Now, bae, you know me better than that."

Malcolm said, "All my grandpa used to say was 'when the cat's away, the mice will play.'" He said the difference between most cheaters and their accusers is just one of them got caught, and the other one haven't been caught yet.

Lisa said, "Yeah, man, listen to your own advice. You're probably all the way on the other side of the world somewhere. You better not be out there cheating on me and your wife with none of them other hoes who are there on vacation too. Malcolm smirked at that thought as it played out in his head. It was funny because he knew that she was right on point with her theory of him. He dared to be tricked and led to that topic of discussion, though.

He said, "Alright, Lisa. I gotta go before I get caught on this phone."

She didn't want to let him go, she now knew what Patti LaBelle was going through when she sang "love need and want you, baby" to her man. But she also didn't want him to know that he had a hook in her mouth. She said, "Okay, bae, I love and miss you, and can't wait for you to get back next week."

Malcolm callously shot back, "Love you too." Then he hung up. She sighed long and hard.

She said, "Damn, 'love you too.' It's not the same as I love you. I bet you he tells that hefty bitch he's married to, 'I love you.'"

Malcolm walked over to a bathroom stall in the men's room on the cruise ship he was on. He then bent down and slid the small cell phone up under the stall to one of the members of the cruise ship crew. Malcolm saw the crew member in the bathroom on the phone and offered him $20 dollars to allow him to make a five-minute phone call on it. Malcolm then turned and left the men's room and headed back out to re-join his wife at the morning breakfast buffet. The kids were still in their rooms in their beds sleeping. His wife had already fixed her plate and was seated out in the large dining area, waiting for Malcolm to return from the bathroom so that they could say grace and enjoy their meal together.

He walked over to the table where his wife was sitting and bent down and kissed her on the cheek. He then reached down and picked up his plate and eating utensils, and headed over to the buffet area to fix his food. He then noticed that Lisa's observation was spot-on. There were a lot of attractive women on vacation, on this cruise right now. Eyes were all over the room, you just had to know how to look without staring and be a little discreet, that's all. He discreetly peeked back over his shoulder at his wife, to see if she was watching him. She wasn't, she was looking at one of the many magazines that the cruise ship had sitting out for the passengers. Malcolm walked up behind a very thick attractive lady who was already in the buffet line. They both made brief eye contact, acknowledged each other with a nod of their heads, then they both looked down at the food selections the buffet was offering.

Then on cue before any one of them said anything else to each other again they both scanned the room to see if anyone was watching them slightly interact with each other. They both were professional cheaters, skilled in the art of deception. Without looking up at her, Malcolm asked the attractive female where she was from. Without looking up, she told him she was from Lake Wales, a small city in Polk County Florida, and scooped eggs onto her plate. Malcolm said, "Oh, I'm from close around there. I'm from Florida too."

She said, "I'm originally from Tampa. My man is from Lake Wales. I moved there when I met his crazy ass."

Malcolm said, "Why you talk about your man like that? Where's he at anyway?" He was asking her that more out of fear of her man catching him talking to her, than genuine interest.

She said, "Oh, he's in the room sleeping. That's all he's been doing since we came on this cruise four days ago."

Malcolm said, "What you want the man to do? He is on vacation, right?"

She said, "He could've stayed his ass at home and slept."

Malcolm had set his trap. Now he was about to bait it. He said, "What is it to do out here on this ship besides sleep?"

She said, "There's plenty of things—gambling, fucking, drinking, eating, swimming anything other than just always sleeping." She didn't know it, but she could have shut up right there and stopped talking. She had said the magic word: *fucking*. He looked up at his wife who simultaneously looked up from her magazine for a brief second and smiled at him. He smiled back. He grabbed a pen sitting on the buffet table and quickly scribbled his name and phone number on a napkin. She was hesitant to take the napkin at first, acting like she wasn't interested. So Malcolm reached and grabbed the tongs that were used to grab and sort the bacon. He glanced over at his wife once more, and took another try.

He slipped his hand in his pocket, pulled out a huge wad of cash. Pulled a hundred dollar bill off of that, grabbed the napkin he had scribbled his name and number on, then pushed them both back towards the female. She grabbed them both smoothly and quickly without much more convincing, with the sleight of hand of an experienced, trained magician. And just like a magic trick, she made them both disappear into her bra-less bosom. And then just like the two seasoned, trained cheaters that they were, they slid past each other with loud enough for everyone to hear matching "excuse mes" to each other. Relaying to anyone who may or may not have seen or heard anything, that they were no more than strangers passing through on a ship. Which was true minus the fact that they had exchanged personal information, privately.

The cheating heart—the main area on the body where people in love claim they place the person they are in love with. Then they do this type of crap on vacation on a cruise ship, with their two significant others not far away. The girl took her food and went back to her room to a Rip Van Winkle-esque boyfriend who, she failed to tell Malcolm, had worked several doubles at his construction job so that he could save up the money to continue to pay all of the bills at their house, and still afford to take her on a nice vacation.

He had paid for this whole vacation, but she was complaining behind his back, not being appreciative and telling half the story. The half that made him look bad, not her. Malcolm's no-good ass went back over and joined his faithful wife.

Back in Orlando Lisa was walking around her house searching high and low for a bump of powder. She was walking around her house looking like one of the characters dancing behind Michael Jackson in his *Thriller* video. Looking in places and in rooms that she hadn't even been in for quite some time. She was desperate, though; she really didn't know what kind of addict she was until now. When Malcolm was around, she never had this problem. As a matter of fact, when he was around, she didn't really have any problems. For right now she just needed a bump of cocaine to get her over. Damn, she couldn't wait a whole week until he got back. She was looking everywhere hoping that somehow Malcolm had been careless and dropped or left a baggie of Snow White somewhere. That would definitely be a fairy-tale ending.

Chapter 4

SIMPING AIN'T EASY

PERVY PAUL HAD AN ENVELOPE stuffed full with cash. He and his friend Judge Jude had just left Chili's meeting with one of the wardens. Jude had headed home to his wife, and Pervy Paul was thinking about doing the same thing, but having that thick envelopes stuffed with cash was giving him other ideas. He was heavily thinking about calling the "Obama" phone of a particular young lady, whom he paid handsomely to do perverted things to him. The extra money that he made every two weeks from his illegal and corrupt side hustle allowed him to operate unfettered by his wife when it came to money and finances. He never had to go into their joint bank account and take any money out. To throw her off his trail, though, from time to time he would have her withdraw him $200–$300 here and there.

He preferred to use the money he got paid every two weeks to do his tricking with. He had a safety deposit box filled with money for when and if his wife ever left him. They would go to divorce court and give her half of what he made and saved as a principal. She wouldn't get any of what he was sneaking and storing in this safety deposit box. It was just so crazy to him that he and his wife had stood before a judge and made vows to each other that neither was hardly and willingly fulfilling. On top of all that, he was actively playing a major part of a criminal conspiracy with an actual presiding judge to get sensitive information from students through intel, spying, and confidential private conversations with the students and their caretakers.

He had done a whole bunch of unethical, unprofessional, underhanded, unbelievable things. That's why he sought out this young, fine sweet thang on her Obama phone, every two weeks. Cause without her helping him release some of the stress from out of his life, he truly believed he'd come undone. That's how he had the phone number to Janay's Obama phone anyhow. He had kept the phone number to one of his former students that used to attend the school that he's still principal of now. The girl whose name is Tati lived in Reeves Terrace Apartments back in the days and attended Howard Junior High with Janay before the controversial school board decision. Tati later ended up at Pervy Paul's private school in Altamonte Springs, where they began and carried on even after Tati's departure.

Once Janay and Tati found each other again years later on social media, they talked on the phone all the time. Tati told Janay about Pervy Paul and the disgusting things that he would pay her to do to him. And Janay decided that she wouldn't mind getting in on receiving some of that easy money from him too. Tati also introduced Janay to this new way to trick and make money on this site called Backpage. Yeah, Pervy Paul was going to go home, right after he called that Obama phone and placed him an order of some of that sweet brown sugar he liked so much. Why should he race home to a wife who wouldn't and couldn't make him feel good sexually anymore.

His wife wasn't at home watching the clock on the wall waiting for him to get home. She left him alone to do damn near as he pleased, because she felt that it would be hypocritical to complain and call him out on his sins and shortcomings and not confront her own. She had an extreme gambling addiction and no money. That's why she left him alone and wouldn't confront him about his demons, because confronting him about his may somehow also expose hers. Her husband made a lot of money being a principal, and it went straight into their joint banking account. He never bothered her about the account, except for every once in a while having her withdraw a couple hundred dollars for him. She had free rein over the account to do as she pleased with money that he worked for and earned, not her.

This was a classic case of "those that know don't care, and those that care don't know." Hell, naw she wasn't gonna bother her nasty, perverted-ass husband. Cause she damn sure wasn't gonna perform whatever disgusting thing he was out there in the streets trying to get some other female to do to him. She was waiting for nine o'clock to strike so that she could check her Florida Lottery tickets. Pervy Paul came back outside of the building where his safety deposit box was stored. He had four crisp blue-face $100 bills inside his pocket. The rest of the bulging stuffed envelope was safely put away. He walked back to his car and got in and dialed the numbers to her Obama phone. A sweet voice came on the line, "Hello. This is Baby Phat."

Chapter 5

JACKSON CENTER REUNION

Janay was at home getting ready to go to the Birthday Bash that she had seen posted all over town on fliers, and broadcast on the local urban hip-hop radio stations. She had seen those fliers yesterday when she went down to 3-N-1Hair Salon when she went down there for her hair appointment with Mrs. Vette. She had seen those fliers all over the Crosstown area—at Jean's Breakfast spot, all around the new Soccer stadium, on P&D grocery store, Sunlight Grocery. It was broadcast seemingly all day on the popular local radio stations. Her appearance at this venue was cemented when she stopped by her old neighborhood, Tarver Court, to pick up her son Lil Twan.

When she got to her mama Lisa's house to pick up her son, she was told that he was over at the Jackson Center with his Uncle Jarvis. Janay didn't go inside the house; she stood out on the porch because she didn't wanna have to deal with her mama's aggravating-ass man Malcolm. Nylasia came out on the porch and hugged her big sister and told her where Lil Twan was. Janay walked across the street, passed by Big B's cornerstone, crossed Westmoreland Drive, passed the baseball field that led to the parking lot of the Jackson Center. Where she ran into an old familiar face. Right there picking up trash and keeping the grounds of the Jackson Center clean was a man who had been doing this exact same thing, since she was a little girl coming here.

His name was OJ; he was from Lake Mann and he was a lifelong die-hard J-High Tiger. He had graduated from J-High around the same time the Miami Boys invaded Central Florida, but was one of the smart ones who never got involved with them. He started working for the City of Orlando a year or two after graduation, got his foot in the door at the Jackson Center and decided to never leave . OJ had been around for so long, He even knew Malcolm's trifling ass. They were both around the same age. They both started working for the City of Orlando around the same time, but they were like oil and water, two totally different people. He smiled that dimpled smile when he spotted Janay walking through the parking lot. When she spotted him back, they both laughed, spread their arms as wide as they could open them and embraced each other.

It had been a long time since OJ had seen Janay. He had watched her grow up right across the street in what most people in Orlando called Beirut. The older Janay got, the less he had seen her over the years. He had watched her, her sister Nylasia, and their little brother Jarvis running and playing as children at the Jackson Center.

OJ said, "Hey, girl how have you been doing?"

Janay said, "Good, Mr. OJ."

OJ asked, "How's your mama Lisa doing?"

"She's doing good," Janay lied. But OJ already knew this, you don't work right directly across the street from a neighborhood named after some killing fields on the other side of the world for twenty-plus years, and not hear, see, and know things.

OJ said, "Well, tell her I said hello." He then asked, "What you doing here today? I'm pretty sure your membership has expired." Always the jokester, they both burst out laughing. He said, "Come on in here.

I'll go and find your brother and your son, but first I want you to say hi to some old strangers." They went inside the Jackson Center and right there sitting in a spot that she had been holding down for years was Mrs. Stacia. Mrs. Stacia hadn't been there as long as OJ, but she wasn't too far behind. She, just like OJ, had seen all of the kids in the neighborhood grow up. Stacia jumped up and quickly came around the sign-in desk and gave Janay a huge hug.

She asked both of her old mentors if Lil Twan had been behaving himself while up at the Jackson Center. Both Stacia and OJ, stern disciplinarians in their own right, looked at her and shook their heads no.

Janay, then speaking to the both of them in a matter-of-fact way, said, "Well, my mama trusted the both of y'all to discipline me when I was a young child. I trust the both of y'all to do the same with mine." They both shook their heads in unison, agreeing and understanding, without saying another word. As they were standing there reminiscing trying to turn back the hands of time, a crew that had been together and had been coming to the Jackson Center together for back as long as the H-Boys had changed their name to the Beirut Boys. The Senior Citizens workout crew of Mr. Butch and his wife Mrs. Lydia, Mr. Joe, Mr. Carl, Mr. John, Mr. Charles, and Philly came walking up to the sign-in desk so that they could go and do what they had been signing up to do for close to twenty-five years—work out.

They all took their time signing in, respectfully spoke to everyone, and then made their way down to a room that had probably helped to extend their lives a number of extra years at this point. Janay said hello back to all of them and made a mental note to try and do like them and take her health more seriously in the near future. OJ walked to the entrance of the computer room, which was about fifteen yards away from the front entrance and the front sign-in desk where Janay and Stacia we're standing chatting.

Janay could hear Mr. OJ say, "Jarvis, hurry up. Lil Twan's mama is here to pick him up." Hearing that, they both came running out of the computer room. Jarvis came out first with his lil' five-year-old nephew hot on his heels. Janay noticed how her little brother had grown to just as tall as her now. He was growing up on her right before her very eyes; only problem was is she hadn't been paying attention. She had heard that he was hanging with some kids who were stealing cars, carrying guns, and moving funny. But she was also told that he was a little pretty boy who was just a follower. She also knew that he was a fourteen-year-old teen going through growing pains, in a dangerous high-crime area, where his dad sold drugs, and fed them to his mama.

Janay knew then that she had better keep a closer eye on her little brother, try to make and spend some time with him, see where his head was at. She had Shayy Dawg watching and keeping tabs on him too. He was the leader of the Beirut Boys. He most definitely wouldn't let Janay's underaged brother join his syndicate. Then came running up her Son-shine, her one and only child, Lil Twan. His father Twan was in Federal Prison doing 188 Months (fifteen years and six months). He and his longtime homie and best friend B Plate had been convicted and sentenced two and a half years ago. His bestie B Plate had been given 221 months (eighteen years and four months).

They had gotten sloppy. They had made a lot of money together in the streets. Protocols were ignored, rules were broken, strange new faces were allowed around to conduct business. They had been hit with a conspiracy charge, and a delivery charge. B Plate started messing around with this girl from Clermont, which was his personal business. B Plate had an old lady at home, the girl from Clermont was involved with and had a baby by a dude in the NFL. Still none of Twan's business. That was one of the great things about their friendship—they pretty much stayed out of each other's personal business. But many times best friends or close friends don't make good business partners, because it's the stuff that we ignore, that is the stuff that hurts you the most.

The girl from Clermont that B Plate was seeing on the side wasn't only cheating on her baby daddy the NFL player, she was seeing many different men in different cities. She cared about the NFL player, because he was a great provider for her and her child. But she loved thugged-out street boys who got their money out of the streets. One day when the NFL player was out of town playing a game. The girl from Clermont was pulled over in a car with a big-time drug dealer in the NFL player's home city. It wasn't even her car that was pulled over, and she wasn't driving. A large amount of drugs was found in the vehicle. The narcotics unit that pulled them over called the DEA, who came in and ran her name and background, found out that she had a lot to lose, began to work their magic and manipulate the system to their advantage against her.

They threatened to call the NFL player on the girl from Clermont and tell him all her sordid little sneaky business. For fear that he would cut her off and file for court ordered custody of their child, the girl from Clermont started looking for a simpler solution to get out of the trouble she found herself in. She started telling and giving the narcotics agents information about drug dealers in different cities and states. One of the drug dealers she gave information about was B Plate. Long story short, she set up B Plate who unknowingly walked Twan right into a conspiracy case. The conspiracy charge carried a ten-to-life low-end to high-end sentencing guidelines. While the delivery charge carried a five-to-forty low-end to high-end ratio.

They made a deal to plead out to the delivery charge if the Feds dropped the harsher conspiracy charge that carried a lot more time. B Plate had told Twan that he knew the person that the girl from Clermont had brought to them to purchase a large amount of drugs. But he didn't know the person because if he had, he would have known that the person was a DEA agent brought in to make a controlled buy from Twan and himself. The girl from Clermont wore a recording and listening device when she and the undercover DEA agent came to Orlando from out of town to make the major buy for the Federal Government.

In exchange for setting up Twan and B Plate they let her go and took her drug-dealer friend she had been just riding with instead. Twan and B Plate would later learn while in prison, while reading their motions of discovery sentencing transcripts, that all the girl from Clermont had to do was keep her mouth shut, and her composure. It wasn't her car, she wasn't driving, so it would have been hard to prove that those were her drugs. Too little, too late. Janay went to see Twan three times a month and made sure to take Lil Twan to see his father twice a month. Twan was doing his time at nearby Coleman Medium. B Plate was doing his in Edgefield South Carolina.

Janay had already booked her next week's visitation for her and Lil Twan. She always sent him some money for commissary, and for him to put some on the phone. She always wrote him and sent him updated pictures of herself and his son. Twan was a life-long Crosstown resident who was from a large family called the Ironman family, that most people from Orlando knew or heard about. Over the years they had moved and spread out all over Orlando. But back in the days, they were mainly in the Crosstown, and Downtown Parramore areas of Orlando. They were well known because there were a lot of them. There were so many sisters, brothers , cousins, nieces, nephews, aunts, and uncles in the Ironman family that when you got into a fight with one, you usually had to fight the whole family, because once the punches were thrown and the licks were passed, those damn Ironman family members seemed to start coming from everywhere like ants.

A lot of Twan's many family members would try and keep tabs on Janay for him, but you can't keep tabs on what you can't hardly see. Twan didn't know that Janay was tricking for money on this strange new Backpage phenomenon thingy. She told him she was a bottle girl at a prominent upscale nightclub near Orlando. He took her at her word. Janay walked her son back to his grandma's house to gather up his things. Her son ,just like her little brother was growing up right before her very eyes too. He had never met his grandfather Spoon and his own father Twan was doing a fifteen year Federal Prison sentence. Which meant three things, since Oscar had gotten considerably older.

1. He didn't have the main men responsible for his existence in his life.

2. He would be a grown man, an adult when his father got out.

3. Janay was gonna have to hold him down, protect, and raise him all by herself in a society that pushes child support on one end, and mass incarceration on the other.

Chapter 6

EASTSIDE STORY

JANAY AND TATI WERE GETTING dressed and ready to go to the Birthday Bash in East Orlando. Lil Twan was fast asleep, his babysitter for the night had fixed Shepherd's Pie, fed him, given him his bath, and he had fallen asleep on the floor in front of his TV watching *Teen Titans Go*. Tati had frequently hung out and partied a little on the Eastside of Orlando. That's why Janay was glad that Tati had agreed to go to this Birthday Bash with her. Tati was even familiar with the area that the venue was being held in. While they both were getting dressed a phone began ringing. They both stopped doing what they were doing long enough to investigate which one of them was getting a call.

It was Janay; her Obama phone was ringing, and that meant money. Only clients had that number. It was her trick phone. That's how she knew it was money calling. Tati went back to getting dressed. Janay went to see who was trying to spend money on her. She walked over to her bed and picked her phone up and on the screen it said PPP. That was code for Pervy Principal Paul. She had everyone logged in her phone by some incomprehensible code that only she could decide or remember. If she were to lose the phone, someone steals it, or it ever falls into the hands of law enforcement, then they would blow a blood vessel trying to figure out if PPP was the Payment Protection Program, or if it was a person.

Tati looked at her partner in crime and asked, "Girl, who's that?"

Janay said, "It's that nasty principal you hooked me up with a couple years ago."

Tati said, "You ain't got time to be dealing with him and those strange requests, do you?"

Janay said, "That's just it, Tati. Depending on what he wants done to him this time, I may have more than enough time. He's the one trick that never asks for sexual intercourse. It's something disgusting, pervy, nasty but not time-consuming, and besides he pays and tips well." Tati agreed with her friend's assessment, mainly because she knew that what she had said was truth. Hell she used to trick with Pervy Paul the Principal herself. She was the one who had introduced them. He used to blow her phone up and call her all the time too, but he was really into dark meat, which Janay had and she didn't. She wasn't jealous, though; the man liked what he liked. He had the right to spend his money however and on whomever he chose. She still had a phone filled with Backpage clients too. One monkey don't stop no show.

Janay answered her phone. "Hello this is Baby Phat." Twenty-two minutes later she was pulling into the parking lot of the Smith Hotel in Eatonville. She was a regular customer there, so a lot of times she would call before arriving and reserve a room. She got out of her car and swung by the reception desk to pay and pick up her room key. Then she went to the room and waited for his arrival. Thirteen minutes later, he was knocking at the door. She answered the door wearing the Dominatrix outfit he had paid her extra to purchase and wear. She let him in with a whip in one hand, and a wooden paddle in the other. She whipped and paddled his bare butt beet red for seventeen minutes, and choked him for another five.

And just like that in under thirty minutes she had made $400. He paid her, thanked her for taking his call, and told her he would be in touch again real soon, and disappeared out the door like a smooth criminal. Janay called Tati back and told her to be ready because she was on her way, coming back to pick her up.

Tati said, "I know that's right, girl. Went and made that quick easy money."

Janay said, "Yeah, you already know. Get ready to come outside. I'll be there in about ten minutes."

Tati said, "Girl, what did that nasty man want done this time?"

Janay said, "The usual. Be outside when I pull up, and I'll tell you all about it when I pick you up."

Less than thirty minutes later, they were pulling into the parking lot of the club where the guy was throwing his Birthday Bash. Janay had gone over all of the sordid details of her session with Pervy Paul. These two friends had always shared sexual stats and statistics like two former old teammates. They got out of the car and headed to go and see what all the hype from this Birthday Bash was all about. Although there was no entrance fee, being that it was a Birthday Bash and all, they still found that the line leading up to it was long and barely moving. The main reason it was moving slowly was because security was doing pat-downs and running the metal detector wand over everyone entering.

Once Janay and Tati made it through all of the formalities, the music was blasting, the partygoers were dancing everywhere, when Janay and Tati made their way around the club, they saw why. Known Orlando mega DJ Disco and the City Boys were spinning the beats. Disco was one of the only familiar faces at this party to Janay, though being that she was from West Orlando. It was almost as though she had traveled out of town to attend this party. This Birthday Bash had been well advertised with the radio ads and well-placed fliers and all, because it was wall-to-wall packed with good-looking, attractive women and men. The event was catered so there was food everywhere. The only thing the patrons had to pay for was drinks at the bar. After dancing to a couple of songs out on the huge, active dance floor, that's where Tati and Janay headed.

It wasn't photoshopped, he looked good just like on the fliers. He was behind the bar talking to a dude who had several cases of expensive name-brand liquors on a moving dolly. He was apparently pointing the dude in the direction of where he wanted him to set the expensive liquor down. He was the guy whose face was on the fliers, and he was the guy who everyone was obviously here to celebrate his birthday with. He had on a nice gold and all black Crooks & Castles outfit, a very expensive-looking gold Cuban Link chain, with the exact same matching bracelet on his wrist. He had on custom-made all-black Jordan's, with the Nike swoosh painted in gold.

Janay and Tati both discreetly nudged each other the way two friends do when they wanna make sure that they both are seeing the same thing, and they're both in agreement. Tati leaned over and whispered, "Damn that man is sexy" in Janay's ear.

Janay leaned back over and said, "Yes, girl, I second that emotion."

Janay ordered herself a cup of Ciroc, and Tati ordered herself a Casa Migos. They made their way back over to the dance floor. They were having such a good time. This was different for Janay, She wasn't used to hanging out like this. Especially after she had low-key started placing ads on tricking on Backpage. She hadn't hung out or went to a club-type environment to try and have some type of social life since before Twan went to prison. Being that he was her man, she wasn't about to be out here in these streets embarrassing him. That's why she didn't even go to clubs or parties on the Westside. His family, the Ironman family, from Crosstown was so big and knew so many people, she knew that she was bound to know somebody that knew somebody that knew somebody. Plenty of the dudes at this Birthday Bash tried to push up on Janay and Tati. It just seemed like fools lose their damn minds and home training when some new woman comes around.

Janay tried to keep the hounds at bay by telling them that she had a man and was just there to dance and have a good time. Tati did the exact same thing, but they would have been better off bringing shock collars to this party, cause the dogs were getting off the chain. But what these men at this party didn't know or realize, was that these two females were hustler's just like them. They weren't interested in exchanging phone numbers, getting to know folks or forming lasting relationships. They were here to find suckers who liked to spend that cash. The men thought that they were hunting the women, but not these two. They were hunting the men.

A specific type, though, the married or engaged, flashy, flirty talkative type. They were hunting glorified sponsors. The dudes who tried to mack them and impress them the most were the main ones that they were trained to avoid. Those dudes tended to be the stingiest. The married men, engaged men, and men in long-lasting relationships, were usually the ones who didn't want to lose their fairy-tale lifestyles that they had with their significant other. See, most of the men in this Birthday Bash had come out to party, dance, and have a good time for a few hours with naïve, vulnerable women who they could have sex with, exploit, tell as many lies as they wanted to, and use.

Little did these men know that there were two women in the crowd who played by the same rules and used a similar handbook as them. There were many women at this party who probably felt impressed by and to just be around all of the nicely dressed, handsome, good smelling ballers that they were around tonight. But not Janay and Tati; it was duck hunting season for them and they had plenty of ammunition. That's what females called dudes who easily came up off of money for talk, sex, or sexual favors. There were way more tight-pocketed ballers in this crowd tonight than loose-pocketed ducks. But that wasn't gonna be a problem for Janay and Tati because they both knew how to spot what they were looking for.

They were both standing back at the bar getting themselves another round of drinks, when two dudes dressed similarly—red flag. Both with a Mr. T starter kit of jewelry around their necks—red flag. Approached them at the bar. One of them who seemingly did all of the talking for the both of them—red flag.

He said, "What's up, ladies? How are you two fine-looking specimens doing tonight?" *Specimens*—red flag.

Janay spoke up and said, "What is a specimen?"

He lied and said, "Oh, that means fine." Truth is he had heard that term on an old 1970s blaxploitation movie and had decided to use it on the next chick he ran into.

Janay said, "Oh, I'm definitely fine, but I don't know about her," she added, pointing at Tati. "You'll have to ask her yourself." He stood there dumbfounded, looking as if he were a comedian standing on stage who had told a funny joke to an audience that didn't catch the punchline.

He tried again, saying, "What are y'all dinking tonight?" He pulled out a large wad of money—red flag.

Tati spoke up this time, saying, "I'm drinking Cash Migos. You'd have to ask her what she's drinking." The dude was now seemingly getting visibly offended. He felt like a ping-pong ball that these girls had now volleyed back and forth.

He quickly put his money back in his pocket and said, "What's wrong with y'all hoes? Me and my boy was just trying to be nice and get to know y'all."

Janay looked at Tati and said, "Well, that's strange cause your boy never said anything. You're the one doing all of the talking. Your friend must speak sign language and read lips."

The silent friend then spoke up and said, "Man, see? I told you that they looked like bougie bitches before we came over here, forget these stuck-up hoes. Let's go." The talker nodded his head in agreement and the wonder twins disappeared into the crowd like trained escape artists.

When they were sure that they were gone Tati said, "Hey waaaaiiit. We didn't catch your names," and her and Janay burst out in laughter. Tati said, "Girl, you is so crazy," as they continued cracking their sides at what had just happened. "Girl, that dude looked like he had money."

Janay said, "Yeah, but I could tell that that loser wasn't gonna be coming up with anything. Girl, I counted at least five red flags, and you know what the experts say."

"'Don't ignore the red flags!'" they both yelled in unison. Janay said, "Girl, that mofo was so tight that when he walks he squeaks." They laughed again; they were truly having such a good time. They sipped their drinks, and then Janay said, "I was skeptical of him when he first walked up. Any man that comes out with all of that jewelry on display, he and his homeboy, are truly trying to impress. Those two tag-team women. When they go somewhere together they look for a woman who has a friend with them. I bet those fools have multiple baby mamas that hung together."

Tati said, "Yeah, that was weird how one did all of the talking for the two."

Things were beginning to wind down. Disco had announced last call for alcohol an hour ago. He had played three straight slow songs, and the last one was playing now and people who weren't dancing were headed out of the club. Then all of a sudden the dude whose face was on the fliers, the one who had thrown this Birthday Bash came out to Disco's DJ booth and grabbed the microphone. He thanked everyone for coming out and making his birthday celebration a success. Everybody remaining clapped for him, sang Happy Birthday to him, and then started heading for the parking lot. Janay and Tati were almost out of the exit when Janay felt a tap on her shoulder. Janay slowly turned and was about to dismiss whoever this was trying to shoot their shot at the last seconds like a buzzer beater. But when she turned around her eyes made contact with the hand of the shooter. She immediately changed her mind. It was none other than the Birthday Boy himself.

Chapter 7

THE FEDS ARE WATCHING

ONE OF THE REASONS WHY Shayy Dawg was so good at his role as leader of the Beirut Boys was because he was seldom seen. That was one of the reasons why he ran a "no social media" rule for all active members of his gang. The Boys in the fishermen's hats and sneakers were a street gang, but they operated more like a business. The members worked shifts in and around Tarver Court and Crosstown, and got paid every week. During Shayy Dawg's five years of leadership of the Beirut Boys the Feds had hit and dismembered many other gangs, cliques, sets, or groups of individuals in many different areas of Central Florida. He had managed to keep the

Beirut Boys flying under the radar by having them all dressed similarly, and keeping them off social media.

Shayy Dawg had sat back over the years and noticed how that when the social media fad took flight a few years ago, criminal convictions went up around the country. To him social media wasn't just a local, regional problem it was a global, cultural one. He saw that ever since social media came about, the jails and prisons stayed filled. Shayy Dawg was young, but he had sort of an old soul. His thought process was more in tune with the mindset of a much older man. His father had been given a life sentence when he was a very young child, around five to six years old. So he hated and detested snitches. His mom had married a man in the military she met at The Rainbow Nightclub in Eatonville, and left Shayy Dawg in the house that she had grown up in as a child on Quill Street with her mother.

Always big for his age, other kids found out real quick not to try him. He was also pretty good in sports, but with the lack of an active male role model in his life, he never really stuck with any. He started navigating the tough streets of Tarver Court at an early age, joined the Beirut Boys at thirteen, and by twenty-one had become their leader. He had five high-ranking trusted members who he was close to; that's it. He dealt with them and them only. He called them his lieutenants, and he had them deal with all the rest of the many different ranks of soldiers in fishermen's hats and matching sneakers. The lieutenants always joked that he was the "Where's Waldo" of gang leaders. Cause, they would joke and say, only he knows where he will pop in next. Today he has popped up in Jacksonville, Florida at a University of Florida Gators football game versus the Georgia Bulldogs.

Shayy Dawg is a big Florida Gators football, basketball, baseball, and track and field fan. He secretly attends games all the time. He's there at the game with his cousin who had graduated two years earlier from the University of Florida. Shayy Dawg had paid for his cousin's tuition and eventual education. This is what I'm talking about when I say that he was a savvy businessman. He had put his cousin through college at his favorite school, where he graduated and earned his criminal justice degree.

After graduating a year earlier, his cousin had applied for and successfully landed a job at the Sheriff's Office as an Information Security Analyst. There, he sat around all day looking at and sending sensitive documents and paperwork. He kept his cousin Shayy Dawg abreast of all warrants, arrests, indictments, pending arrests, and indictments and also their new social media cyber surveillance. He would inform Shayy Dawg on when someone was a confidential informant, snitch, cooperating, or fugitive. He kept him up on court dates, subpoenas, and bond amounts. He paid a hefty price to get how far he had gotten; he knew that it was necessary, though, if he wanted to make it further. That's also why he insulated himself in such a way to protect himself and the infrastructure of the Boys in the fishermen's hats and matching sneakers.

The score was tied up 10–10 at the half. He was excited because the Gators got the ball first in the second half and were diving down the field. Shayy Dawg said, "Alright, Gators! It's feeding time, let's eat!" His cousin had brought and shown him some important papers and documents that at the time wouldn't be public record. All of the official members of the Beirut Boys had continued to be loyal soldiers and weren't under any active investigations. But there was someone who rented space, who frequently came around Tarver Court who was in some eye-popping paperwork, working as a confidential informant. Shayy Dawg knew what must happen next. He was gonna have to send some troops to see him.

The Gators had moved the ball all the way down to inside the Bulldogs' ten yard line. He was pumped, he was excited he had bet a lot of money on this game.

The very next play, the Gators' Quarterback dropped back to pass the ball; his receiver had beaten his defender, had a whole step on him. The crowd looked on with anticipation, everyone including Shayy Dawg jumped to their feet. The Gator Quarterback let it fly; the Bulldog safety stepped in front of the wide-open wide receiver and intercepted the pass and ran it back 98 yards for a 17–10 Bulldogs' lead. Half the crowd had their hands on their head dejected in disbelief, while the other half was jumping up and down as if they had hit a scratch-off ticket.

Shayy Dawg couldn't believe his sudden change of fortune. He said, "Damn, cuz, did you see that crap?" He pointed his baseball glove-sized hand at the scoreboard at the replay of the Georgia Bulldogs' highlight reel play. The crowd was especially loud all game long as two neighboring states that are known for and great at football took heavyweight title swings at each other on a football field. The Feds were watching and doing a roundup soon, but none of those likely to be indicated were Beirut Boys. He and his cousin parted ways and drove back to Orlando separately in two totally different directions. No one knew that they were cousins, and they planned to keep it that way.

Chapter 8

IT WAS SO CRAZY THAT IT HAD TO BE TRUE

IT WAS COMING UP ON the last semester of school. This was very important from a timing standpoint, very important to Jude and Paul. It made both of their jobs a little more difficult with the kids being out of school. It was especially harder for Paul because he was a principal at a private school. Not as hard for Jude because kids got into trouble all the time. It's just that during the summer, it's harder to lock kids up on loitering and truancy. But they both had received a very important phone call earlier in the week from a representative of the wardens. They both had been summoned and were on their way to a weekend meeting with them in Ocala. These clandestine meetings didn't bother Jude or Paul, because they always concluded with an envelope filled with cash. The meeting spot this time was a Hilton Inn, where they all met in a huge conference room.

When Jude and Paul pulled up a few minutes apart, they walked into the conference room together, and it was already filled with all of the wardens of the private prisons, work-release centers, juvenile justice centers, and work camps. They were all seated around a big circular conference room table. Each one of them had an assistant or two with them. When Jude and Paul made their way into the room, they both found seats around the large conference room table. Once seated, the warden from the Ocala work-release center motioned for his assistant to start the seminar. He walked around the room and handed everyone in attendance a stack of stapled papers that were filled with charts, bars, and graphs.

They were told that the paperwork was a comprehensive study of the activities of youth between twelve and twenty-one years of age, during the summer when schools and colleges are out for the summer break. If Jude and Paul hadn't realized that these folks were dead serious about keeping these facilities filled, they did now. The paperwork stated that they were using algorithms about these young people's tendencies to tip the scales of justice in their favor. Jude felt a little uneasy looking at this statistical cheat sheet. He had gotten these illegal activities because it seemed to be safe, easy money at first. It seemed to him as if they had gone from asking him to jump rope, to asking him to bungee jump, with no safety net. He wasn't a chance taker, at least not like that. He was only a few years away from retirement. He could lose everything that he had worked all those years for.

The charts, bars, and graphs didn't bother Paul in the least bit. He felt perfectly okay with anything and everything, just as long as the envelopes filled with cash kept coming. They could have asked him to do just about anything, just as long as he got to continue moonlighting as a principal, just as long as it didn't stop him from being around all of those pretty young girls. Not only was he willing to bungee jump for those "envelopes filled with cash giving" wardens, he was willing to do it from an airplane, over shark-infested waters. He was the ultimate thrill-seeker and until the wardens came up with this opportunity for him, he'd had a pretty boring life, and he had to spend his own money seeking thrills.

Jude, on the other hand, still seemed to have some semblance of a moral compass, and the charts, bars, and graphs forced him to take a long hard look at what exactly he had gotten himself involved in. He had been sitting on that bench, judging and making life-changing, life-altering decisions on other people's lives. Now here he was thinking about what would happen to him if he were to get caught. If the tables had all of a sudden turned and he was standing before the judgment seat, instead of sitting in it. Paul, on the other hand, was excited for this opportunity to further this criminal enterprise he was involved in. He was so afraid that this paid joyride would end soon, but these charts, bars, and graphs were a sight for sore eyes.

The Ocala warden's assistant gave everyone in the room a detailed breakdown of everything on the charts, bars, and graphs. After carefully listening, Jude and Paul both realized something. Jude realized that he had gotten in over his head, and was gonna look for a way to back out of this and disassociate himself from these people. Whereas, Paul was determined; he was gonna happily help try and put more bodies into the beds at the private prisons. To him this was clearly a supply-and-demand situation, and he planned on supplying what the wardens had in charts, bars, and graphs demanded.

After the meeting was over, all the paperwork with the charts, bars, and graphs was collected by the same person who had passed them out. He made sure that everyone turned their paperwork in; then he walked over to a large shredder and shredded all of the damning evidence concocted by an elite group of community leaders. The paperwork was destroyed in front of everyone to ease any worry and anxiety of that type of data becoming public. They adjourned the meeting and on their way out, Jude and Paul were both handed envelopes filled with cash. They shook all of the wardens' hands and headed their separate ways, both with smiles on their faces. One of those smiles was of an excited, happy man who had just been given a large amount of money, and an assignment that could help him make a lot more. The other man had a forced smile on his face, one where you had to smile to keep from crying.

Jude was shaken by the depth of the corruption he had allowed himself to become involved in. He badly wanted to talk to someone who could help him get out of this quicksand he had fallen into. But who could he tell about this and not end up in handcuffs and on breaking news? He had too much to lose and that just wasn't a chance that he was willing to take. Besides, who could he tell that would actually believe that a judge, who had judged, sentenced, and incarcerated others, had allowed himself to be involved in something so sinister? No, he wasn't about to tell on himself, he and the Paul and the wardens had been very careful this far. He lived in a society that looked at things, not into things. He also knew that once you reached a certain level or status in this social-media-driven society, that not many people did much research.

Jude shook Paul's hand as both of them made it back out to their cars in the parking lot. He couldn't believe that he was selling young teens and young adults up the river for cash incentives, but he had an envelope stuffed with cash sitting on his passenger seat as evidence against those thoughts. People came in his courtroom all the time babbling off fake news gathered off of social-media sites. But he also knew that only 21 percent of people actually did their own research of things. The rest sat around watching these twenty-four-hour news stations that pandered to the senses of whether the viewer is a Republican or Democrat. He liked those numbers, and he loved his chances of not getting caught. People were so gullible now they had an actual TV show on called *How to Get Away With Murder*. He pep talked himself right back into the mix. He was retiring in less than four years. He wouldn't be caught, or stopped. He knew that only real eyes, realize, real lies.

Chapter 9

BEWARE OF DAWG

ON THIS DAY SHAYY DAWG is making a business decision, but this was nothing new to him. Running this corporation called the Beirut Boys had not been easy, but he had been chosen to make the tough, hard decisions. It's lonely at the top people would always say. He never liked that saying. *It's crowded at the bottom is more like it*, he thought. He had come from the bottom and worked his way to the top. He was not trying to go back down the ladder that he had grinded so hard to get to the top of. He had gotten his hands dirty to get to where he was, and on many occasions he had gotten blood on them when necessary. It had been necessary a lot lately. The paperwork that his cousin had bought to Jacksonville and shown him, almost guaranteed bloodshed.

He called out his hit squad, a special group of natural-born killers dressed in fishermen's hats and matching sneakers. Today they're sitting in the apartment of one of their homegirls named Allison, whom they grew up with in Tarver Court. Allison wasn't home, but that was okay. Shayy Dawg had let himself in. Being that he was the leader of the Beirut Boys, he had spare keys to many different domiciles in Tarver Court, Crosstown, and the 32805 area code. He only let his lieutenants know when he had arrived and called and told each and every one of them to come and meet him at Allison's apartment.

Thirty minutes later sitting there in Allison's kitchen was none other than Trick, TT, Lil Richard, and Funk. These were four of his five lieutenants who worked exclusively under Shayy Dawg. Shayy Dawg trusted them all with his life and freedom. They had been his childhood friends and had come up through the ranks with him. They were very loyal to him and did much of the heavy lifting when it came to sending and delivering messages. They dealt with the lower-ranking members and Shayy Dawg paid them very well to help him keep things in order. Many of their fathers, uncles, older brothers, and cousins had been members of the

H-Boys. Trick was the wise, cool, calm, and collected one who spoke a lot of knowledge. But once he realized that he couldn't reason or talk with you, he would become unreasonable and violent.

One time when he was a student at J-High, rumor had it that he walked into the boys' restroom and confronted some members of a rival gang. He then placed his briefcase on top of one of the bathroom sinks, popped it open and pulled out a long Clint Eastwood in *Dirty Harry*-looking .357 Magnum and said, "Whoever's got beef, bring it to the Butcher." TT was the youngest of the lieutenants and he had earned his stripes in the beginning by doing B&E burglaries. Back in the early days when the Beirut Boys had started making a name for themselves, they didn't have all of the new firepower of automatic weapons in their arsenal that had become customary in the streets.

They were raising Hell with revolvers, shotguns, .22 and .25 small caliber automatics. When TT joined, the Boys in fishermen's hats and matching sneakers became weaponized. He used his spectacular cat burglary skills to break into pawn shops, gun stores, and gun shows. The next thing you know the Beirut Boys were armed like a small militia. TT was also a ladies' man. He had run through so many different females Crosstown that he ended up getting several of them pregnant, many of them at the same time. He was so notoriously whorish that rumor had it that he made so many children in Crosstown that every park he drove by, he should throw his arm out the window and wave, just in case a couple of the kids out there were his.

Lil Richard was only a year older than TT, but he was the most trigger-happy and looney of the crew. He started out as a jackboy who was involved in several violent home invasion robberies, but he was also known to do brazen broad daylight stickups as well. He was feared in the streets, by drug dealers, other robbers, night-drop money couriers, and gambling houses. If Lil Richard was seen in any particular neighborhood besides Tarver Court, word got out and spread like wildfire. Shayy Dawg had taken him in as a favor to one of the old fallen soldiers who was one of the original members of the H-Boys. His name was Pop and he was the Uncle of Lil Richard. Shayy Dawg was skeptical of bringing him on at first, because he was a robber and a renegade. But now, after a couple of years of being Beirut Boys together, he was glad that he had taken the chance on the young fella.

Funk was the quiet one who showed up, did what needed to be done, and then disappeared just as quietly as he had come. He drove all different types of vehicles all with dark tinted windows. He was hardly seen hanging out anywhere other than Tarver Court. It was rumored that Funk had never been to a party, a nightclub, stores, malls, or weddings—anything or activity that included a large crowd. But he could tell you almost anything that happened at them. It was almost like he had eyes in places that his body wasn't.

Shayy Dawg and the lieutenants sat around the table in Allison's kitchen. Shayy Dawg pulled out a cell phone and passed it to his left to Funk. Funk took it, looked at whatever was on the screen, looked over at Shayy Dawg, nodded his head in agreement, and then passed the phone to Lil Richard. Lil Richard looked at the screen, looked at Shayy Dawg, nodded his head in agreement with a smirk on his face, then passed the phone to TT.

TT took the phone, looked at the screen, then said, "I knew something wasn't right about him," nodded his head in agreement, and passed the phone to Trick. Trick took the phone looked at the screen, nodded his head in agreement, and then slid the phone back to Shayy Dawg. No words were said or exchanged after that. The lieutenants had seen what they needed to see. Shayy Dawg got up first and headed out the backdoor entrance of Allison's apartment.

As he was going out the door, he said, "The last man out, lock the door." The lieutenants understood the assignment. The meeting was adjourned.

Chapter 10

WE CHECK PAPERWORK CAUSE PAPERWORK DON'T LIE

THAT EXACT SAME NIGHT, A dark blue Suburban that could pass for black pulled up to the back parking lot of a popular well-liked nightclub called A Touch of Class. A Touch of Class was right up the street from Tarver Court on Parramore right smack dab in the middle of Crosstown. The owner of A Touch of Class nightclub was one of the original Miami Boys, who had arrived in Orlando with the first wave. His name was Gee and he and the Beirut Boys had a mutual respect for each other. Gee had stayed in Orlando and made it his permanent residence. He was extremely smart and business-minded, used his money from his drug proceeds to first open a Game room/Record store. Although he was still in the streets getting money, he owned and operated a legitimate business as well.

After a couple of years, he stepped his game up and got into the nightclub industry and ended up with one of the best nightclubs in Orlando. TT got out of the Suburban and walked up towards the backdoor entrance to the club. This entrance was mainly used by Gee and his employees to enter and exit. It was Friday, skin-to-win night. Skin-to-win is where several girls come to the club in a private setting and undress and get naked for cash incentives. Inside the skin-to-win contests, it wasn't unusual to see money exchanged for sex or sexual favors.

TT and the other three lieutenants knew that the man they were looking for would be there. They knew that his kryptonite and main weakness had always been women. They knew that he had always pretended to be this suave "Don Juan type" character who had the gift of gab when it came to getting women. But truth be told, he was a pillow-talking paymaster who would tell a female what, when, where, and with whom her man was cheating, just so that he could take a shot at her. He had spilled secrets told to him in confidence by some of his closest friends to the women they were dealing with. Now it had come to the Boys in the fishermen's hats and matching sneakers' attention that his homies weren't the only people he was snitching on.

The photos on Shayy Dawg's phone showed that he was a paid confidential informant working with the Feds, the Sheriff's Office, and the Police Department. He had been going out of town making controlled buys for all three agencies, while being wired up and filmed. He may have even gotten away with it if he would have just stayed in jail and did a little time. But when you're a whore with whore problems, jail ain't the place to be. He stayed in jail for less than three months on serious charges that included several direct sales to an undercover agent. Several sales and delivery charges, he had an unlawful use of a communication device where they recorded several drug deal conversations with him. And on top of all that, he was hit with the R.I.C.O charge—which Black folks call "your Mexican cousin that you don't want to meet."

R.I.C.O is an acronym for (racketeering influenced corrupt organization) and was mainly used to infiltrate and bring down the big Italian Mafias of the '70s and '80s. Over the past twenty to thirty years, they have been also used to infiltrate and bring down street gangs, cartels, corrupt police departments, and corrupt politicians. Due to these particular situations, Shayy Dawg had spent the big money investment of putting his cousin through college. His cousin was the one who had explained to him how the Mafia had always used a comprehensive approach to being infiltrated by law enforcement, rats, and snitches. He said the Mafia knew that most criminals, especially drug dealers, used nicknames, most people in the streets didn't know their real government name that's on this birth certificate.

In order to join those Italian Mafia groups, the members had to bring their birth certificates, ID, and pertinent family information, so that the Mafia could dig into their backgrounds. The applicant's real birth names were on those documents that they turned over to the Mafia, which meant if their names popped up anywhere in the system, being that most paperwork is public record, all the Mafia had to do was send someone down to the Clerk of Courts, pay $2 per page for the paperwork, and find out just what the person with the catchy nickname was up to when he thought no one was looking. That's how they had stumbled across the man the four lieutenants had a seek-and-destroy meeting mission with Shayy Dawg about earlier in the day.

If Shayy Dawg and his cousin had only known him by J-Spot, his nickname, then his freedom could have become costly to the Beirut Boys. Shayy Dawg's cousin was a very valuable secret weapon. He had done research and dug and found a case out of Lake County, Florida that had ties and connections to Orange County. When he did a little digging, he started going through the real government names in the arrest report records and stumbled onto an old Thirty-Third Street arrest photo of one of the guys arrested in the Lake and Orange County drug bust. The cousin compared the new arrest photo with the old one and found out that Jerome Fenton was a fool owned by the police.

TT knocked on the backdoor entrance to A Touch of Class. One of Gee's security team members who was working the back door that night, looked out of the peephole of the big metal door and saw TT's familiar face. He knew that TT and Gee were cool, so he opened the door and let TT in. TT was also a frequent face on Skin-to-win Friday nights. As TT came in through the back door, he dapped the security guard up.

"What's up, bro? Are they in there?" he asked, finding out if the usually large crowd of women and men were in the Boom Boom Room, where it all goes down.

The security guard said, "Yeah, T, they down there. It's some fine new ones in there too."

TT smiled and said, "Well, I better get my Black butt back there and see what you're talking about then." He took off, headed for the Boom Boom Room. He turned and asked the security guard, "Hey, bro, is Gee down here?"

The security guard laughed and said, "Is a pig's pussy pink?" They both laughed as TT kept walking. TT got down to the Boom Boom Room where there was another security guard at that door. Gee had it set up that if you came to Skin-to-win Friday, you weren't coming to just watch. If you weren't getting naked, then you were spending money on someone who was. The security guard fist-bumped TT and let him in. He felt right at home here. He was in one of his comfort zones, in the Boom Boom Room around a whole bunch of gyrating, dropping it like it's hot, twerking women who were shaking what their mamas gave them. He didn't mind that some of the Skin-to-win contestants had belly fat, bullet wounds, and BBLs. He didn't mind the scars, the makeup or the lace front frontals either.

He was a camel-toe connoisseur, and if they were lacking in the back but packing in the cat, they were alright with TT. He looked around the room and saw a lot of the usual crowd of dudes who almost always showed up every Friday to throw money at the girls just like him. He saw his homegirl Big Beirut in there who may as well count as one of the guys. She dressed like a dude, she looked like a dude, talked like a dude, fought like a dude, and loved looking at fat coochie prints like most dudes. She was sitting there dressed in a fishermen's hat with matching sneakers, getting a lap dance from a fresh new face. He then spotted Gee in front of this chick who was in town from Decatur, Georgia named Jane Mignon who had skinned all the way down to her thong. She obviously had Gee's undivided attention, because for at least five minutes, he didn't look to the left or the right, nor up for that matter.

TT knew that the lil fine-ass Jane chick had Gee mesmerized, because for the same five minutes Gee was stuck, he was stuck watching her from way across the room too. As he kept looking around the room he spotted the man who would have been on a wanted dead or alive poster if they were in an old cowboy country western. J-SPOT was preoccupied with a sexy, sweaty, gyrating light-skinned chick from New York, but had moved to Orlando named Thugdoll. She was slim-thick with tats everywhere and she showed up at Skin-to-win Fridays at least once a month. She'd go back and forth from Orlando to New York, but she now called Orlando home. Even when her mom, sisters, and brothers moved back up north, she decided to stay. Gee finally looked up from Jane Mignon popping her pelvis in his face. He saw TT standing to his right, shot him a thumbs-up, and turned his head back around quickly as he gazed upon Jane's birth canal.

Then J-SPOT looked up and locked eyes with TT. They both nodded their heads at each other the way down South dudes did each other, when they didn't want to yell all the way across the room at each other. The song went off and J-SPOT stood up from his seat in front of Thugdoll and waved a bunch of money he had in his hand at TT, as if he were waving him over. TT put up the "hold up for a minute" finger, letting J-SPOT know he would come over in a few minutes. He then pulled out his cell phone and sent out a group text: the player is here everybody get in position. He put the phone up and walked past Gee, who had literally kidnapped Jane Mignon and was holding her hostage inside of a crowded room filled with people. He dapped Gee up as he walked past him and his kidnap victim. He made it all the way down to where J-SPOT was with Thugdoll. They reached out and dapped each other up. Just another Skin-to-win Friday at A Touch of Class; it was booming in the Boom Boom Room.

Chapter 11

GO FEED MY FRIENDS

AFTER HAVING A FEW DRINKS and a slew of lap dances in the Boom Boom Room at A Touch of Class, TT and J-SPOT were having a good time doing what they seemed to love the most, being in hoes' faces. Gee allowed a lot of things to go down in his establishment. Folks had been caught having sex inside, giving head inside, fighting, snorting coke, and even sleeping. Almost anything illegal that you could name, people had been caught doing it there. But the one rule that Gee did enforce was no smoking, cigarettes or weed. He couldn't stand the smell and would get physically sick at the smell of both, but especially cigarettes. TT and J-SPOT both liked and respected Gee. They had gone outside to TT's

Suburban to smoke a blunt. On the way out, TT had told J-SPOT to hold up he had to take a quick leak.

While J-SPOT waited for him outside, he stepped into the men's bathroom pulled out his cell phone and sent out a group text: On my way out bae. He quickly peed and stepped back out in the hallway where J-SPOT was waiting where he had left him. They were sitting inside of the Suburban passing the blunt back and forth talking about America's team, the Dallas Cowboys. The both of them were huge Cowboys fan, and they, just like every other Cowboys fan, were saying that this was gonna be their year. They both said that with confidence, even though neither one of them had even been potty trained when Michael Irvin, Emmitt Smith, and Troy Aikman led Dallas to their last Super Bowl win in 1995.

Another group text went out, but this time TT wasn't the one who sent it. It said: Sitting Duck. TT looked at his phone and then went right on talking about the Dallas Cowboys. He passed the blunt back to J-SPOT. Another group text went out, and his phone vibrated again. He looked at it again, and this time it said: Go feed my friends. TT and the other three lieutenants all knew who that text had come from, and they all knew what it meant. Knowing what that meant, TT changed the subject.

He hit the blunt again, and as he was passing it back he said, "Hey yo, man, why the hell do they call you J-SPOT?"

J-SPOT inhaled the exotic strand of weed they were smoking, exhaled, and said, "Why do you think, fool? Cause I be hitting them hoes' J-SPOT." TT laughed at him as if he had given a stupid answer.

He said, "First of all, dummy, what you're talking about is called a G-spot. Second of all," he said with a serious look on his face, "that's a slick way to hide who you really are Jerome Fenton."

J-SPOT looked at him as if he had just pulled his ski mask off during a robbery. He was in the middle of saying, "Hey, man, how the hell did you kn—" when all of a sudden, three doors on the Suburban flew open all at once, all except the driver's seat where TT was sitting. Three masked men dressed in all black and armed with automatic weapons appeared out of nowhere.

One of them said, "This is a jack-move. Don't make it a homicide." J-SPOT quickly put his hands in the air visibly shaken up. He was looking even more perplexed when he glanced over at TT who seemed to be totally unfazed by the three gun-wielding assassins and the whole ordeal.

J-SPOT nervously said, "All right, man, we'll give y'all whatever y'all ask for just please don't shoot us." He was talking to any of the gunmen who may have been in charge. He was so scared and nervous it seemed like his mouth contracted diarrhea. He said, "What did we do, man? We didn't know that them were y'all's women," pointing back at A Touch of Class.

Lil Richard chimed in, saying, "Man, you've got mo' problems than hoe problems."

Trick spoke up next, saying, "Give me your phone and your car keys." J-SPOT quickly handed them both over.

Then TT, still sitting in the driver's seat with his hands up over his head said, "I got a question." He very slowly lowered his hands 'til he reached down between his driver's seat and the center console and came back up with a Glock 27, that he pointed at J-SPOT too. "Police-owned fool, did you think your paperwork was safe?" J-SPOT was numb. He knew that they had him dead to rights, or wrongs, if we're being technical. His worst fears had come true. He had been exposed.

On all of those undercover drug buys that he had been on and made for the Feds, the Sheriff's Office, and the Police Department, he had backup and protection if things were to get out of hand and go south. But not now. Where was his backup? He had gone out of town and set people up plenty of times. He was actively working with three different branches of law enforcement in Orlando, trying to make his charges go away. He had done what they secretly signed him up to do. They had come to him while he was in jail several times offering him deals to be a confidential informant. He was scared at first, but jail wasn't for him.

He was having trouble with his wife, and his hoes. His hoes were talking, telling what he had been up to and the gossip was getting back to his wife. He had to get out. He signed the paperwork to become a CI. The agents told him to go back and do the same things that he had been doing when he got busted and arrested. He started making controlled buys for them. They swore to him that he wasn't in any danger. He needed them now to save him, to protect him, to remove him from harm's way, but where were they? They had told him things that led him to believe that no one would find out that he was a rat. Where were they to end the threat and bring him back to safety? He had committed the ultimate street sin. He had helped take a lot of men off the streets, broken up their families. All of this in an effort to try and stay out and save his.

Some say that street rules are stupid and unfair, but that's usually after they get caught and it's time to pay the hefty price, that they signed up for freely and willingly. If J-SPOT had not agreed to become a rat and work for the Feds, the Sheriff's Office, and the Police Department, he would have simply gone away to prison somewhere and did some time. But with him signing his name to be a paid confidential informant he had agreed to join forces with the same people he was happily making a lot of money being their backs. That's how rats and snitches justified their actions. Instead of after getting caught just facing whatever time law enforcement is going to give them, they just turn rogue traitor and join forces with them fighting crime. He had avoided a prison sentence, but was now facing a life sentence from some guys in fishermen's hat's and matching sneakers who administered street justice without favoritism.

TT said, "By the way, Jerome, get your police-owned behind out of my front seat," all while still pointing his gun at him. He said, "Get your butt back there in the back seat where you personally put plenty of brothers." J-SPOT moved quickly, jumping down out of the passenger seat while Lil Richard and Funk stood close by with their weapons of war aimed at him. After J-SPOT slid into the back passenger seat, Lil Richard climbed in to the front passenger seat. Funk walked around and slid into the back seat behind the driver's seat, and they closed and locked all the doors. Trick walked around to the side parking lot, where all of the club patrons parked their vehicles. He pulled out the keys he had taken from J-SPOT, he then started pressing the key-remote. The headlights flashed on a 2016 black Ford F-150 truck.

Trick jumped into the F-150,.cranked it up, put it in reverse and backed it out, then pulled around behind the other three lieutenants and their prisoner. They pulled out of A Touch of Class's parking lot, turned right onto Parramore, drove down a block and a half to Anderson, made a left, then drove down Anderson and got on the I-4 ramp headed towards Daytona. Both of them successfully made it onto I-4, with Trick following at a safe distance behind the Suburban so that no one else, especially the police, could get behind them. The four lieutenants had made this trip plenty of times; they all practically knew it by heart.

They were headed eastward towards Sanford. They knew when they saw the sign that said Exit 101C, that was their exit to get off of I-4. They got off on the outskirts of the City of Sanford, the city made famous for where a man doing neighborhood watch followed a Black teen after being told not to do so by a 911 operator, and ended up shooting and killing the teen, claiming self-defense on a controversial "stand your ground" defense, and then being acquitted. They exited and pulled into a very familiar boat dock that circled around and ended up directly underneath the I-4 exit they had just gotten off of. The boat dock that they had pulled into the parking lot of led out to the widespread St. John's River, which is the longest river in Florida at 310 miles long, spanning through twelve counties from Jacksonville to Tampa.

The thing that Shayy Dawg and the lieutenants liked the most about it was that it was alligator-infested waters. The Suburban pulled in with J-Spot's F-150 following closely behind. It was 3:08 a.m., the Witching Hour. In secular lore, 3:00 a.m. is also referred to as the Devil's Hour, which, in satanic circles, is a mocking inversion of the time that Jesus supposedly died on the cross—3:00 p.m. Did these four lieutenants know any of these extenuating facts about 3:00 a.m. or the Witching Hour, the time of night they usually put in their work? Maybe, maybe not.

They stopped both vehicles down close to the boat dock. TT and Lil Richard, both front seat occupants, got out first. While Funk held his gun on J-SPOT, informing him not to move. Lil Richard opened the door behind the passenger seat. TT and Funk came around and trained their guns on him as well.

Lil Richard said, "Let's get this shit started." He stepped forward and ordered J-SPOT to take off the large Cuban link necklace he had around his neck.

J-SPOT said, "Alright, man, you got that. You can have this shit. Y'all just d me man." He pulled the heavy and expensive chain off over his head and shakily handed it to Lil Richard.

"Naw, fool. Put it on me." Lil Richard instructed J-SPOT to put the chain on him over his head the way he had taken it off.

TT stepped up next and said, "I want the bracelet," letting J-SPOT and the other three lieutenants know what he had chosen as spoils of war with his chance. J-SPOT nervously unclasped the matching bracelet to the Cuban link chain he had just placed around Lil Richard's neck. As TT held out his left wrist, J-SPOT looked at him, trying to garner a mustard seed of sympathy from his fellow Dallas Cowboys fan and once-a-week Skin-to-win mate. There was none. After J-SPOT clasped the bracelet around his wrist, TT stepped back, and Funk stepped up.

"Fool, what you got in your pockets?" Funk asked, having already peeped his bulging pockets when he was sitting in the back seat next to him. J-SPOT started emptying his fat pockets, pulling out large wads of cash from at least three of his pockets. He started handing all of the money he had on him to Funk.

TT said, "Damn, that fool spent a lot of money in the Boom Boom Room on them hoes. I picked the necklace because I didn't think he had much money left on him." The last time they had done this Trick had gone first, and that's why he was last today. They went by rotation, a sliding scale rotation.

Trick said to J-SPOT, "You ain't got much else to take. I guess I'll take those rings off your fingers. J-SPOT slid his wedding ring and a fancy nugget ring off and handed them to Trick.

Funk said, "Damn, bro, you taking the fool's wedding ring too?"

Trick said, "The way this idiot be tricking off all over town, he didn't take his marriage seriously anyway."

They then made him strip down to his boxers and took his wallet with his ID and important documentation. Then they all spread out in a box formation and pointed over at the boat dock and told him to start walking. J-SPOT immediately started beg-talking.

He said, "Man, if y'all let me go, y'all won't ever see or hear from me again." He was looking to make a deal to save his ass again like he had done before.

Funk laughed and said, "Yeah, man, we know. If we let you go you gonna tell them folks you been working for on our backs, and we'll all be up shit's creek."

They continued walking, pointing those high-caliber guns on him from four different directions just in case he changed his mind. The closer they got, the more scared and desperate J-SPOT felt. They stepped onto the dock, and he said, "Naw, man, I'll leave the country. I got people in Canada. I'll leave and go there tonight. And won't ever come back."

Then Trick said, "Fella, you're a cooperating government witness. You're most likely on a no-fly list, and you definitely ain't gonna be able to leave the country. Besides if you go on the run from the Feds and local law enforcement, there will be an APB out for you or a missing persons' report within forty-eight hours. Even if you get away for a couple of years, they can catch you two years from now and you could still tell on us, and we could all still go to prison for a long time."

They made it all the way down to the end of the boat dock, where J-SPOT said, "Man y'all just tell me what I need to do for y'all not to kill me tonight." The four lieutenants were all spread out in a straight line behind him. He was at the end of the boat dock; another step and he would be floating in the St John's River. They all looked at each other as if they were pondering how to answer J-Spot's last question. They all looked over the railings of the boat dock where they could hear all kinds of movements, splashing and strange noises down in the dark waters. J-SPOT heard all of those strange beastly noises made by only God knows what creatures were down there, and for a brief moment he thought about taking his chances getting shot. But looking at the caliber of guns he'd get shot with, the number of people holding those guns, and the number of bullets he'd get hit with, quickly made him scrap that idea.

Funk spoke up first, repeating J-Spot's question out loud. "What would you have to do for us to not kill you? Swim fast," and then he fired and shot J-SPOT in the right shoulder. J-SPOT was terrified, but he had nowhere to run. Funk had purposely scraped him. He was leaking and dripping blood. The dark waters really started to come to life and get active. Large beasts were heard rustling and moving around in the dark waters below. He was cornered on a dock, facing a terrible choice of death by firing squad or a watery grave. It was fight-or-flight time, pick-your-poison time. Before he could make his mind up another shot rang out. This time it came from Lil Richard's gun. The shot kneecapped him and knocked him back into the cold dark water.

The alligators we're waiting for him. They had been smelling the blood ever since Funk first shot him. The first wave of alligators was on him in a matter of seconds after he splashed down. The four lieutenants walked over to their ringside seats at the railings and watched a movie that they had seen before. J-SPOT let out a death-shattering shriek as alligators grabbed him from many different directions, and went into their famous death rolls ripping off chunks of flesh that used to be a living, breathing man. In less than four minutes, the dark waters calmed down. The alligators had swum back to their watery post positions, leaving no evidence of Jerome Fenton. He had promised to disappear and never show up again if they were to let him go. They had made him disappear and never be seen again in their own way.

They walked back to the Suburban and the F-150. Trick and Funk climbed into the F-150, while the two young guns, TT and Lil Richard, jumped inside the Suburban. This time they would follow behind Trick and Funk to make sure no one got behind them. Their destination was a car mechanic shop ten miles away on Old Winter Garden Road, where the F-150 would be dropped off. When the mechanics arrived to the shop tomorrow morning, they would take the GPS tracking system off the F-150, get rid of the tags, file off the VIN number and create a fictitious title for it. Two days after, they would ship the F-150 overseas, where it would sell for above market value.

Shayy Dawg and the four lieutenants would all rake in about fifteen grand apiece. J-Spot's phone, wallet, and clothes would all be thrown in a big barrel at the mechanics shop and burned into ashes. And the jewelry that they took from J-SPOT would never be worn by any of them. They had a jeweler in Miami who would burn down the gold that they received from their missions, and make it into something specifically for them. That way they never got caught with some dead person's jewelry. These young men were smart, careful, calculating, and loyal. They were the Boys in fishermen's hats and matching sneakers, who took pride in going to feed Shayy Dawg's friends.

CPSIA information can be obtained
at www.ICGtesting.com
Printed in the USA
BVHW081734130123
656258BV00002B/515